Published in the United States by Forever Young Publishers
P.O. Box 216, Niles, Michigan 49120
Fax: 269.683.7153

Visit us on the Web:
www.foreveryoungpublishers.com
e-mail: cheri@foreveryoungpublishers.com

First Edition
Printed in China through Four Colour Print Group
Louisville, Kentucky

Publisher's Cataloging-in-Publication
(Provided by Quality Books, Inc.)

Hallwood, Cheri L.
One wish for Winifred Witch / written by Cheri L.
Hallwood ; illustrated by Patricia M. Rose. -- 1st ed.
p. cm.
SUMMARY: In this rhyming story, little Winifred Witch
is excited about enjoying Halloween night with the big
witches, but she has one small problem--she is afraid of
the dark. Her secret wish is never to be scared of the
dark again. She asks her Aunt Broomhilda, who owns a
shop of spells, to help. When magic fails, Broomhilda
shows her another solution to her fears.
Audience: Ages 4-8.
LCCN 2010922490
ISBN-13: 9780977442225
ISBN-10: 0977442225

1. Witches--Juvenile fiction. 2. Fear of the dark--
Juvenile fiction. 3. Halloween--Juvenile fiction.
[1. Witches--Fiction. 2. Fear of the dark--Fiction.
3. Halloween--Fiction. 4. Stories in rhyme.] I. Rose,
Patricia M., ill. II. Title.

PZ8.3.H15960ne 2010   [E]
                              QBI10-600050

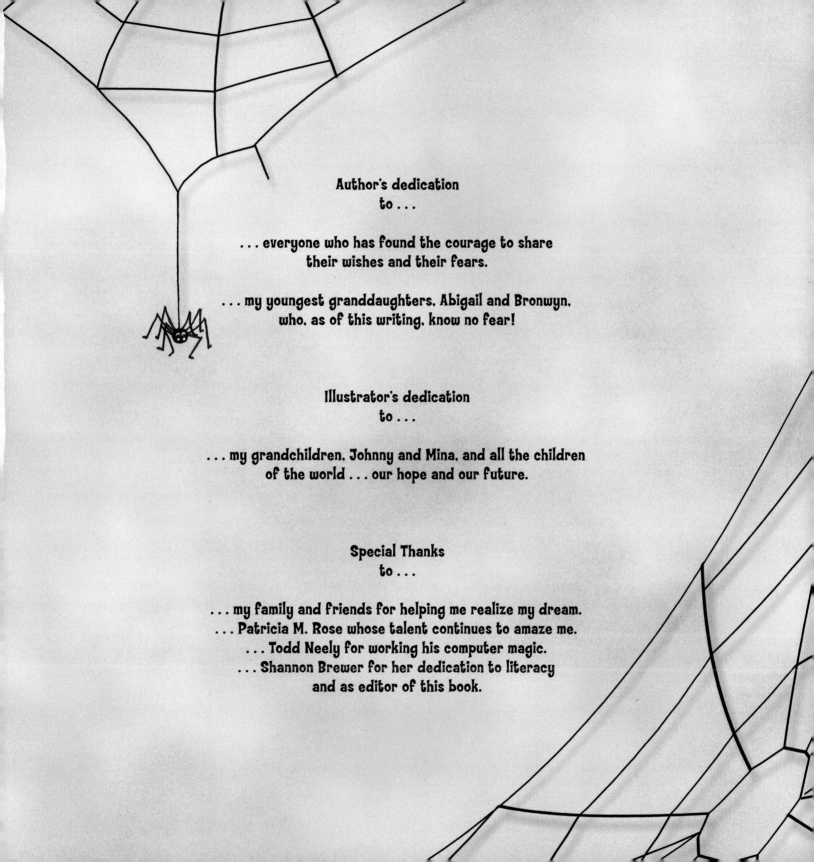

**Author's dedication
to . . .**

. . . everyone who has found the courage to share
their wishes and their fears.

. . . my youngest granddaughters, Abigail and Bronwyn,
who, as of this writing, know no fear!

**Illustrator's dedication
to . . .**

. . . my grandchildren, Johnny and Mina, and all the children
of the world . . . our hope and our future.

**Special Thanks
to . . .**

. . . my family and friends for helping me realize my dream.
. . . Patricia M. Rose whose talent continues to amaze me.
. . . Todd Neely for working his computer magic.
. . . Shannon Brewer for her dedication to literacy
and as editor of this book.

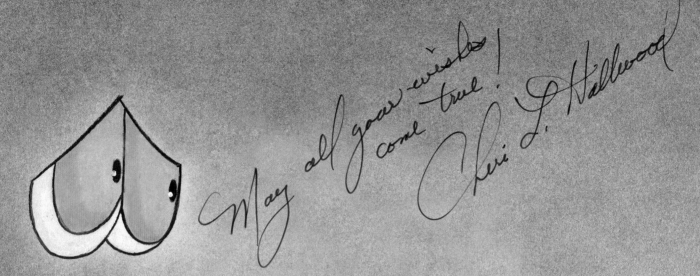

May all your wishes come true!

Cheri L. Hallwood

A book from
Forever Young Publishers
for

One Wish for Winifred Witch

Written by
Cheri L. Hallwood

Illustrated by
Patricia M. Rose

Way down in Haunted Hollow
Soon witches will be seen,
Dancing in the moonlight
For tonight is Halloween.

'Tis the night
for Hocus Pocus,
A witch's Show-and-Tell.

See them gather
'round their cauldrons
And brew a
Magic Spell.

But on this night for Magic, that comes just once a year,

Not every witch is ready, not every witch is here.

For deep inside the Hollow, along Every Witch Way,

Hides little Winifred Witch, on this Halloween day.

Every Witch Way

Now...

She's a good little witch
From her head to her toes,
But there's SOMETHING about her
That NOBODY knows.

You see...

When the sky grows dark
And the moon glows bright,
Little Winifred Witch

Is NOWHERE in sight!

Happy Halloween

Now...

She Loved Halloween!
Everyone knew that she did.
But when nighttime came

Little Winifred hid!

For **No One** knew of her fear.

No One knew of her fright.

No One knew of the

ONE WISH

She would make

Every Night.

I wish,
I wish with
all my heart
to never
again be
afraid of
the dark

NILES

How unfair, Winifred thought.

It just didn't seem right.

A WITCH...

AFRAID of the DARK,

NOT on HALLOWEEN NIGHT!

There must be some WAY!

There must be some HOW!

There must be some ONE,

Woooooooo

Woooooooo

Why Aunt Broomhilda, OF COURSE!
She'll know JUST what to DO!

So she reached for her broom
And out the window she *FLEW*!

Whooosh!

"Broomhilda's Shop of Spells"

Read the sign above the door.

And there stood Aunt Broomhilda, sweeping Spells up off the floor.

Inside the
Shop of Spells,
much to Winifred's
surprise, were
Potions,

Spells,
and

MAGIC BEANS...
Every COLOR,
SHAPE,
and Size!

Could MAGIC BEANS
be the answer,

the WAY

and

the HOW?

Could Aunt Broomhilda be

the ONE

to help her...

RIGHT NOW?

So she whispered quite softly
In Aunt Broomhilda's ear
And told her all about
Her ONE WISH and her fear.

Aunt Broomhilda simply smiled
As she gave her a hug.
Then explained about
such THINGS
While they sat upon a rug.

"You see Winifred...

Being afraid of the dark
Doesn't just happen to You,
It happens sometimes
to Big Witches too.

"I have NO spells or Magic Beans
To make your ONE WISH come true.

But I have an IDEA,

A SOLUTION for you."

Then a lantern of Fireflies
She took from a shelf
And told Winifred she used it
Sometimes for herself.

Winifred smiled bravely,
For Tonight
she would not hide.
She'd fly into the moonlight
With the lantern
by her side.

And so…

Tonight in Haunted Hollow

ALL the witches will be seen,

Even little Winifred,

After all . . . It's HALLOWEEN!